PET?

RON CRAWFORD

PET?

GREEN TIGER PRESS
Published by Simon & Schuster
New York London Toronto Sydney Tokyo Singapore

PET?

COW?

CAT?

BAT?

RAT?

WOW!

DOG!

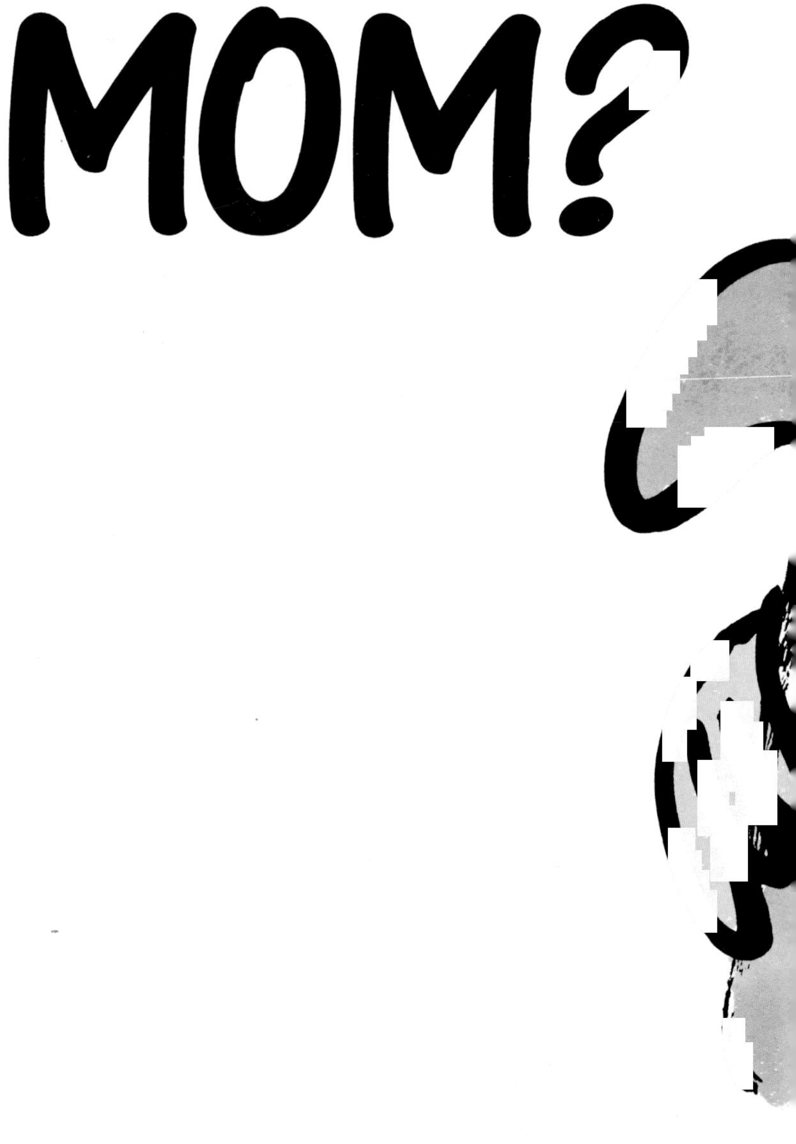
MOM?

NO!

DAD?

NO!

WELL...

O.K.

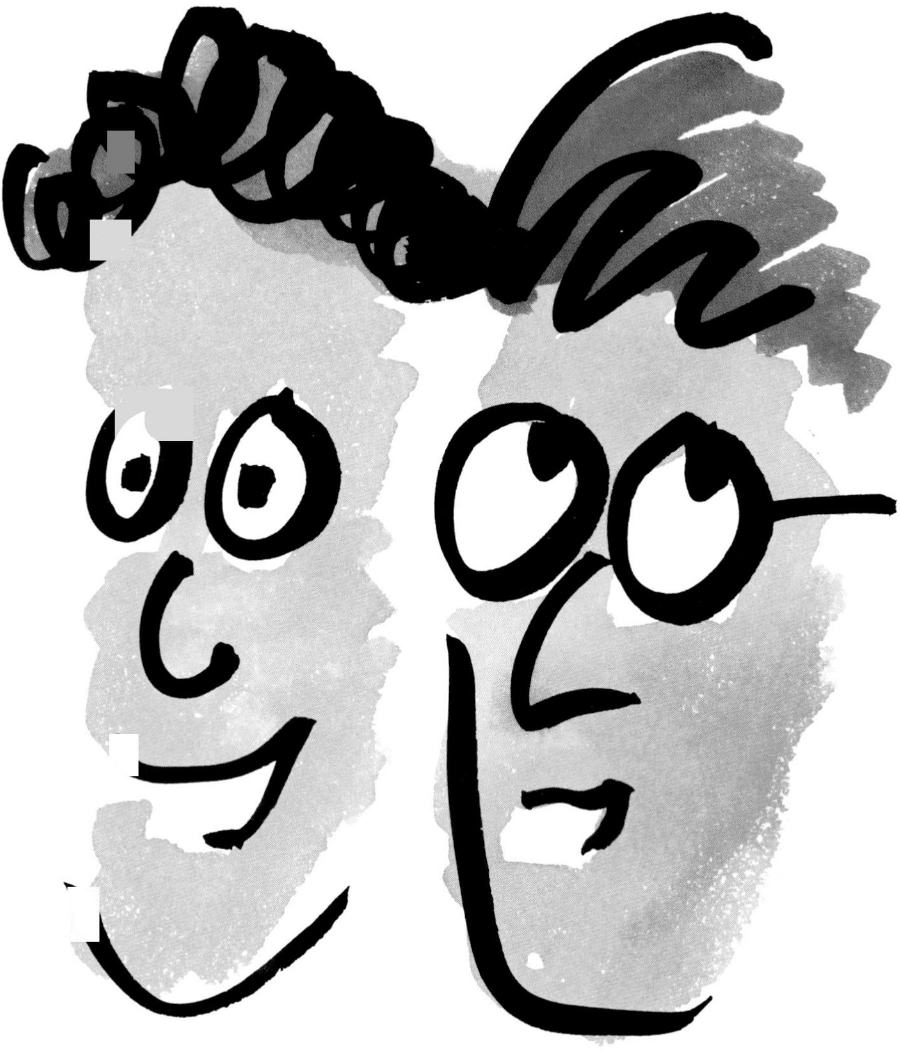

YES!

WOW!

BOW WOW!

GREEN TIGER PRESS
Simon & Schuster Building
Rockefeller Center
1230 Avenue of the Americas
New York, New York 10020

GREEN TIGER PRESS is an imprint of Simon & Schuster.
Manufactured in the United States of America

10 9 8 7 6 5 4 3 2 1   (pbk) 10 9 8 7 6 5 4 3 2 1

Library of Congress Cataloging-in-Publication Data
Crawford, Ron. Pet / by Ron Crawford. p. cm.
Summary: Illustrations with few words tell how a girl
ends up with a dog for a pet. [1. Pets — Fiction. 2. Dogs — Fiction.]
I. Title. PZ7.C85917Pe 1993 [E] — dc20 92-18600 CIP
ISBN: 0-671-79675-5   ISBN: 0-671-79335-7 (pbk)